CIRCUS GIRL

MICHAEL GARLAND

DUTTON CHILDREN'S BOOKS   NEW YORK

Alice is a circus girl. Everyone in her family is in the circus. Alice's mother walks the tightrope, and her father is a clown.

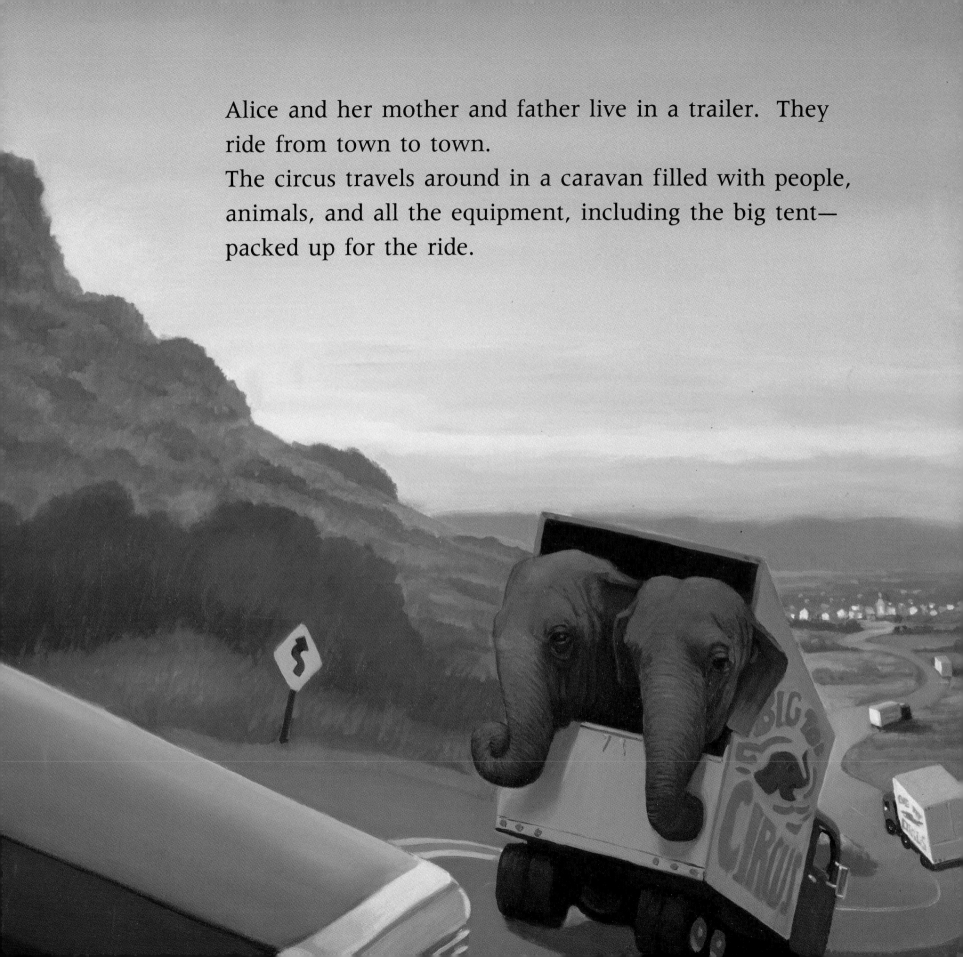

Alice and her mother and father live in a trailer. They ride from town to town.
The circus travels around in a caravan filled with people, animals, and all the equipment, including the big tent— packed up for the ride.

When the circus comes to a new town, the elephants are paraded through the streets. Circus people put up signs and give out handbills to let everyone know when the show will begin.

Before the show, there is so much work to be done. Circus men put up the tent. The performers practice their acts, and the animals are washed and brushed. All the circus people help, including Alice.

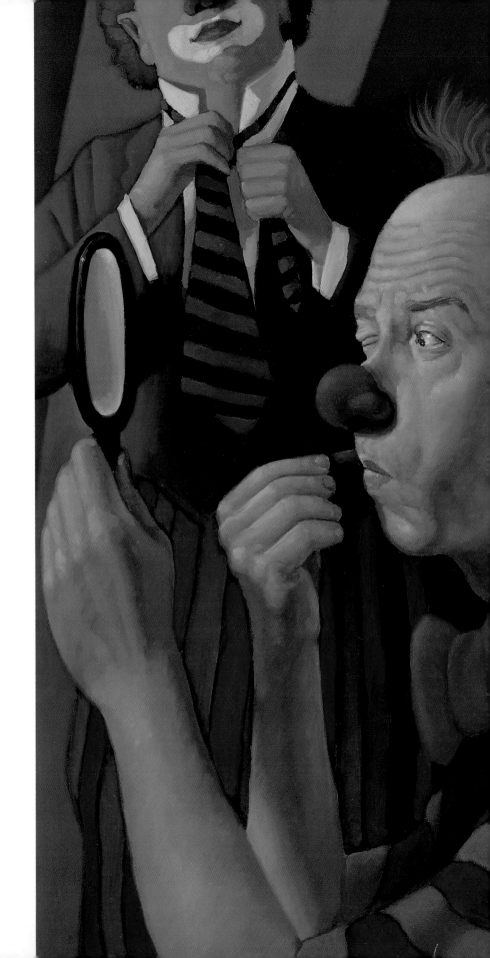

The show people put on their
costumes, and the clowns
paint their faces. Alice can't
decide what she wants to
be when she grows up—a
tightrope walker or a clown.

With a roll of the drums, the band starts to play. The show is ready to begin! The ringmaster, Alice's grandfather, leads the elephants into the big tent, followed by clowns, fancy horses, jugglers, acrobats, and all the others, in a grand procession around the three rings.

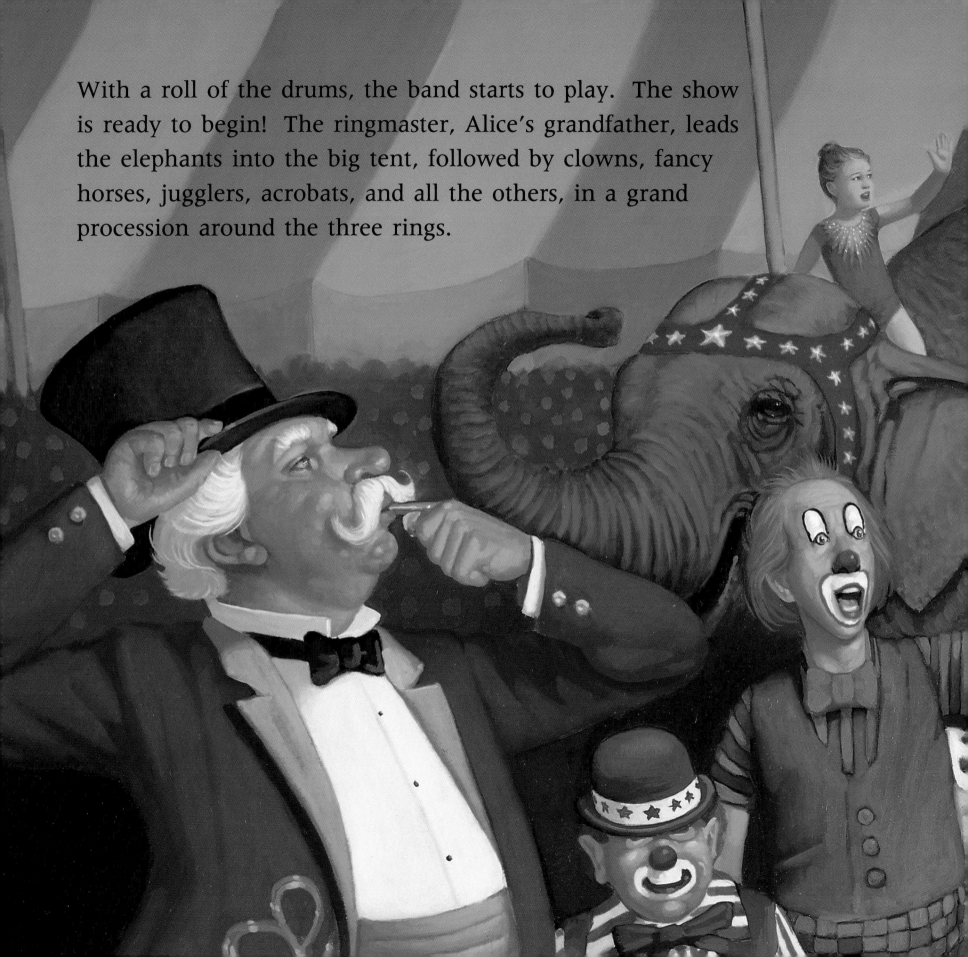

The townspeople cheer!
The children shout!

Then suddenly, the music stops. The ringmaster leaps into the center ring. "Ladies and gentlemen, and children of all ages..." he says in a loud voice, announcing the acts—something different in each ring.

Everyone loves the Famous Dancing Bears. The biggest
bear can even ride a motorcycle!

The Flying Gazpacho Brothers are Alice's uncles. Their skill and balance astound the audience!

Alice holds the hoop for her Auntie Anne's Amazing
Performing Trick Dogs. Alice is so excited!

The lion tamer is very brave. When he cracks his whip,
all the lions and tigers sit up and roll over.

The last and greatest act of all are the elephants. They entertain the audience with many clever feats. And then they lead the closing parade around the three rings. Other circus performers join them and wave good-bye. The townspeople cheer! The children shout! And then they go home.

The rings are swept clean, and the animals are back
in their pens and cages. The work is done.
The hungry circus people sit down to eat the dinner
that Alice's grandmother has cooked for them.

Everyone is tired, especially Alice. Her father reads her a bedtime story before she goes to sleep. Alice has to get up early in the morning because the circus is going to another town—maybe yours!

for Mom and Dad

Library of Congress Cataloging-in-Publication Data
Garland, Michael.
Circus girl / by Michael Garland.—1st ed.
p.   cm.
Summary: Alice and members of her family spend a busy
day working in a circus as it travels from town to town.
ISBN 0-525-45069-6
[1. Circus—Fiction.]   I. Title.
PZ7.G18413Ci   1993
[E]—dc20   92-22270   CIP   AC

Published in the United States 1993 by Dutton Children's Books,
a division of Penguin Books USA Inc.
375 Hudson Street, New York, New York 10014

Editor: Riki Levinson

Printed in Hong Kong by South China Printing Co.
First Edition   10 9 8 7 6 5 4 3 2 1